THE UNFORGOTTEN VOW

REBEKAH SINCLAIR

Warning

This book contains content that may be triggering. Mentions abduction, imprisonment, physical abuse, sexual assault, and torture. Contains explicit language and graphic sexual content.

To: Kim

When you need another perspective...or two.

"For as long as I draw breath, and forever after."

The cliffs at Silver Strand have always been my sanctuary, a place where the relentless churn of the wind matches the chaos in my mind.** Today, like many others lately, I find myself seeking solace, contending with the weight of my thoughts and emotions.

Patroclus, my mate of more than a century, sits beside me, his presence a comforting anchor amidst the storm raging within me. He's always been the steady flame to my wildfire, a balance I both cherish and struggle with.

His icy inferno is both inquisitive and patient. He wields his element with curiosity, using his small tufts of Fire like spies. His Flames roar to intensity when he finds just reason, or sizzles to a plume of smoke when there is none.

I, however, come barreling in Fire first. I'll ask questions after, if anything is left of the ashes, of course. It's what makes me a formidable warrior and a difficult mate.

As we sit overlooking the sea, the waves crashing against the rocks below, I can't shake the feeling of restlessness that has plagued me for the past twenty-two years of our bond. Despite Patroclus' unwavering love and support, I feel like something is wrong, like a link in our chain is missing and we can't fully connect.

A gull caws as it rides the breeze. I watch it balance on the currents of the realm as it hovers above the swollen sea below me.

"Hey," Patroclus breaks the silence, his voice gentle yet filled with concern. "You've been coming here more often lately." Pat lays back on the grass with his hands folded behind his head. "Tell me what is wrong."

There is always a grin on his handsome face, and it matches the playful look in his eyes as he squints against the bright sunlight. A strip of his brown skin shows where his shirt rises above his pants, and I mark his taut stomach with a kiss. Laying back with him, I rest my chin on his chest, I release a deep breath.

I meet his gaze, searching for the right words to convey the turmoil within me. "I don't know, Pat. I just... I feel like there's something I'm missing, something I can't figure out."

Patroclus reaches out, his hand finding mine, a silent gesture of solidarity. "Hey," Patroclus tilts my chin, forcing me to meet his gaze. "I feel it too."

I close my eyes and let my head drift to the side in resignation. As hard as I'm trying to block the storm spiraling in my mind, I can't. I don't want Patroclus to feel as if he is not enough, because he is. Yet, I can't stop this thought that crawls through my mind.

It feels like the slow song of a siren, gently corrupting me so it's all I hear.

"I'm sorry." I'm not sure what I'm apologizing for or why my insides are dripping with guilt. "I love you and– "

"Stop." Pat covers my lips with a finger to shush me. "It's not about me being enough for you or that you are too much for me." Sitting up, Pat bends his knee and pivots so he's facing me. I face the edge of the cliff, hoping these feelings of incompleteness will tumble into the waves below.

"Close your eyes." Pat directs me. While I'm usually the one giving directions, I grin and do as he asks.

That gentle caress against my bond that is my mate, grows in intensity and I take in a shuddering breath. Gently coaxing his seafoam flames through our soul-connection, the sensation travels straight to my cock.

"Pat." I give him a breathy warning and I sense his smile widen.

He leans in closer to my ear, his full lips grazing my lobe before he talks. "Feel me. Feel me moving down our bond." He kisses my ear lightly, moving to my neck.

Against the sensation of his lips on my skin and my dick straining in my pants, I hunt for the stir against our bond and the caress of his element sliding down our connection.

Moving in a corkscrew down the tether that links us, his delicate flames move toward my center. They are widely dispersed and feel uneven as they ferry down the bond.

Pat's hand finds the top of my pants and unties them. Diving under the band, he grips my erection and I buck into him with a hiss.

"Now bring your fire to me." Patroclus makes his way to the other side of my neck, and I lean back on the palms of my hands, giving him better access. His hand squeezes my dick as he runs up the length of me.

"Fuck." I moan when he focuses several pulses at the head of my erection, and I thrust into his hand.

Frosted-green bursts of his aura flare behind my closed eyes as I reach down our bond with my own bronze Flames. Pat moans against my neck when he feels me reach down our fated link.

I match the rhythms of my fire to his and our powers swirl together. Like his, my flames travel down an uneven bond because something is missing.

Someone is missing.

"See, my mighty Achilles." Pat's fires stroke our bond as his hand strokes my dick. My stomach tightens as he works me, bringing me closer to pleasure. "We are not wholly bonded yet, lover."

He picks up the tempo of his movements and I'm nearing the point of climax. I let out a deep moan and he sucks on my neck, marking me as his, forever his mate.

The need to mark him in the same manner rushes through me like a primal urge. Feeling only his hand on my dick and his full lips against my skin is not enough.

I need his body molded against mine. The sensation of his tight ass in my hand with my other tangled in the tight curls on his head. I need to swallow his moans as I taste his pleasure bursting out of him. *I just need him.*

"Pat, I need you," I say, my gruff voice ringing out across the cliff and drowned by the sea. Patroclus was climbing onto my lap before I could finish the sentence. My hands are on him, squeezing him into me as grinds his hardness against mine. Gods, he's fucking perfect.

"Already on my way," my mate answers, just before our mouths collide.

❧ ❧

As we descend from the cliffs, hand in hand, I can't shake the feeling of electricity crackling in the air. Pat's earlier reassurances washed over me like a soothing balm, but I can't shake the feeling of unease that gnaws at the edges of my consciousness.

Tension is a thick blanket that covers the conditioning field as Hermes and Medusa spar, their movements fluid yet charged with underlying frustration.

I watch as Hermes, my old friend, wrestles with the demons he keeps a secret from everyone else. His thoughts torn between his missing sister, Calypso, and the enigmatic maiden who haunts his dreams.

The mention of Calypso's name sends a shiver down my spine, igniting a spark of curiosity that refuses to be extinguished. His sister went missing over two decades ago; along with Delphi's Head Mistress Penelope and Head Minster Odysseus.

Lost at sea, Hermes believed the chaotic wind was telling him Calypso needed help. For days he searched the skies with his Light ability, never finding her.

Each day, the Elementals of Delphi search for the lost siren.

Eventually Hermes located Aphrodite's fleet of ships and discovered Odysseus was captive on her boat. No one thought Hermes could negotiate his release, but the Herald of the Realms did it. After five years of captivity, Odysseus was freed.

Odysseus was locked under the siren's spell and could not recount the events of the storm but confirmed Penelope was alive. Their fated bond was still thrumming within him, even though he could not connect with Penelope through it and find her.

It told us she was living, while likely held within an immortal prison.

If Penelope was alive, Hermes' sister must be as well.

Each time I hear her name, that scratch in the recesses of my mind ignites.

I've asked Hermes to show her to me using his powers of Mirage but it's too painful for him. Recalling the memory of her brings him great grief and he refuses.

If only I could see her face, this curiosity would be satisfied.

Hermes prepares a burst of light and Medusa readies a ground snake. The two Elementals will blast each other at the same time, and neither will likely hit the other.

"Knock him on his ass." Pat calls out just as the two fighters release their powers.

Like a thousand raging tornados suddenly sprang to life, the winds of the realm billow around us. Pat and I hold on to each other's arms and duck low to the ground.

It's coming from everywhere.

Every current of the realm is a raging tempest; angry and in pain, the Winds scream and wail around us.

Hermes is struck in the chest by the force of the wind, and he's thrown fifty feet, sliding the last several yards on his back.

Medusa is cowered low to the ground covering her ears from the deafening roar of the gust.

Trying to make sense of the event, I scan quickly for signs of an attack. The swirl of the wind before me glitters with a golden hue and the form of a being manifests right before us.

The yellow aura of a woman shines like the sun, ethereal and haunting. A long ponytail flows in slow motion on the currents of the raging wind. Wearing a sheer red stola, she reaches her hand out. For a moment, time stands still.

I extend my hand, needing to touch the yellow glimmer before it's rushed away with the storm. Just before I can reach it, it disappears, leaving behind a single word.

"Help."

Ice runs down the length of my body when I hear the voice and it spirals down the bond between Patroclus and me. His head snaps to mine, his eyes blown wide in disbelief.

Looking at Hermes, I find him panting heavily, turned on his side and propped on his elbow. A haunting look of shock covers his face just as it does Patroclus.

"Who the fuck was that?" Hermes' rich blue eyes shoot to mine, and I clench my jaw as her plea rings in my head.

"Callie."

Achilles

For twenty-two years, a silent storm has raged within me, a tempest of longing and despair that can find no solace. But now, standing amidst the aftermath of the windstorm and the chaos of the Commune, I realize the truth that eluded me for so long. The captive woman, wielding the very winds that whisper through the realm, holds the final key to my soul's completion.

Calypso's name echoes in the depths of my being as I lock eyes with Patroclus, my steadfast companion in this tumultuous journey. She is not just my mate, but our mate.

Hermes restrains Odysseus, who bucks and billows in his grasp. Odysseus is in a rage to find Penelope. While he sensed no sign of her during the raging windstorm, the bond is still there. The belief the women are prisoners together grows and the Commune wants to take action to locate them.

Medusa calls Athena through their bond. The great Goddess of War sends a rain shower across the globe in response. She lifts her hands to the skies, and the water held within the clouds drops to the earth. She flings her arms out, and the rains travel away from us, stretching across the realm.

The essence of every Elemental will reside within the molecules of water. Once Athena's spies return to her with information, she'll know where to find them. As Patroclus and I watch the raindrops fall, each one becomes a tiny beacon of hope guiding us in our quest to find our lost mate.

Atlas rushes to the conditioning field, spectacles in hand, his hair disheveled as if the wind threw him around. "It was Calypso." He exclaims breathlessly and Hermes shakes his head in agreement. "Thank the gods." He rests his hands on his knees and works to slow his breathing.

Stalking toward our friend. Pat and I quickly agreed through our bond to keep the fact she is our mate to ourselves for now. Hermes has been missing his sister for over two decades. I know my friend. We'll push him to a point of over protectiveness if we admit this truth now.

"So, what happens? Do we just hope she falls in love with us at first glance?" I ask my mate with a playful tone.

"I mean, I did." Pat winks at me and cocks a crooked grin that makes the dimple on his cheek stand out.

"We're coming with you," Patroclus declares, his voice tinged with determination. With Calypso's beacon casting a shadow over her captors, they must know the Elementals of the realm will be converging on them. There is going to be a fight and there are no warriors more lethal than the three of us on the field of battle.

"It's been three fucking months of searching, Hermes. How much longer will we wait before we go out looking for her?" I nearly scream at Hermes.

"I've been searching for years." He pushes back with a low tone. The dark circles under his eyes tell me his mystery maiden kept him awake last night but I'm losing concern for his secret. I want to find my mate and get her out of the torment she's been suffering in all these years.

Day after day, the Elementals of Delphi search the realm with their powers.

Athena scans the water, Medusa sends out her earth snakes, Atlas scans the minds of the realm and Daphne hunts for emotions.

Patroclus and I stand here actionless, with no elemental powers that can search the realm and we're restless.

"We're leaving tonight. I'm tired of waiting around." I huff at Pat, raking my hands through my hair when an oncoming rainstorm pulls my head to the west.

I look to the east seeing dueling storms rage toward us.

Athena rushes out of the Temple of Apollo and looks at both storm fronts. Raising her hands, the squalls slow and rain falls into each of her hands.

Bringing her hands to her chest and closing her eyes, she takes in the news from the waters. Rain mixes with her tears and both stream down her as she breaks out into a smile. A small fit of laughter tries to choke away the tears as she says the words we've waited months to hear.

"I found them." She looks to Hermes and Odysseus with bright eyes full of hope. "Both of them. They are together and alive."

Pat squeezes my hand in elation, and I release a breath I feel has been trapped within me for more than two decades.

"There are two possible locations." Athena points to the Iberia mountains northwest of us and Seres to the east. "We will send two scouting parties to determine the location. Once we know where they are being held, we meet to plan a rescue."

"I don't like the idea of going in the same group," Pat says to me quietly as the others prepare themselves for the mission. "What if we split up? We can make sure one of us is there with her."

I agree. The idea of not being there when she is found is something we can't allow. One of her mates need to be there to help find her.

Cupping Pat's jaw, I kiss him goodbye. With our eyes closed and foreheads together, we pause with a nervous tension flowing down our bond.

"We'll find her." Pat reassures me.

"I know, just be careful."

"Ready?" Hermes sheaths his swords in the cross-shaped scabbard at his back.

Leaving my mate to join his group, Hermes and I walk to Odysseus.

Keeping my eyes locked on Pat's as he stands with Athena and Medusa, I speak in a low tone to my friends. "If we arrive and the women are at our location, we're not waiting to regroup on a rescue plan, right?"

"Not a fucking chance." Hermes agrees, keeping his voice low so the others cannot hear. "We get them out of there as quick as possible."

The blue light of the portal flares around us and in an instant, the cooler mountain air greets us. As soon as the portal closes, I know we are in the right location. The realm is practically vibrating with her nearness and its as if the very Winds are crying in sorrow at her captivity. The currents shriek between the mountain passes and blow in strong, erratic tufts.

"She's here." I gruff as I look across the mountains that hide in the dark cover of night.

"How can you tell?" Hermes asks.

Keeping our bond from Hermes won't last forever but I can't risk the distraction now. Not knowing we're close. So, I nod in the direction of a bend in the mountain pass where the faint glow of firelight dances on the rocky walls. "Campfires." Surely the presence of others in this remote location is a clear enough indicator.

Sending pulses down my bond to Patroclus, I try to communicate to him that we are okay, and she is here. However, The wards in the area block my ability to communicate with my mate.

"I can't talk to Pat." I let Hermes and Odysseus know as we trudge through the brush and terrain of the mountain.

"That's a good sign for us." Hermes says from the front of our line. Odysseus is in the center, and I watch our backs.

Hermes' Light skips across the rocky floor as he sends a faint pulse of his power out. Odysseus drops to the ground and places a hand on the dirt. With his Earth element, he's checking the area.

We creep toward the glow of campfires. The embers that float into the night sky act as my eyes. Using them to help me map the camp and assess the thermal temperatures of the small army resting in the valley.

There are easily two thousand soldiers here. In a camp above the valley, there is a small group with a high heat signature. Ares has many powerful elementals loyal to him, but one is quite powerful.

I can barely get a read on anything else with the flux of power radiating from the other side of the valley.

The ground is soft and moves under our boots from weeks of rain. I'm still using the burning embers to survey the camp and beg the wind to spread the cinders further before they cool in the air and turn to ash.

As if answering my plea, a rush of air collides with me.

Anguish so deep, it nearly pulls me to my knees.

The campfire embers swirl in a vortex at the entrance of a hand-hewn cave. The door is uneven at the base. It seems slightly bent as if someone struggled and kicked the door askew. Misery pours out of the crack and is picked up by the panicked caress of the wind.

My fires dance within it, eager to speak with me and tell me of the atrocities etched inside the confinement.

I clutch my chest, feeling the pain and shame of my captive mate.

An inferno bursts inside me and tears rush to my eyes with her hurt. She's injured. Gods, the amount of suffering is enough to drown me, and I know in an instant her captives have spent decades breaking her.

But resilience sits steady in her bones, and I feel the fight within her. She's patient and calculated, making me think of Pat. She is a raging tempest of revenge; the same retribution that is fanning the flames of my rising anger.

Calypso is the blend of both of us, our perfect balance.

"She's ahead in a cave." We pick up our pace and follow a worn path that leads to a risen mound of mountain. Below is a valley and within it is the army of Ares.

The door is masked with elemental powers, but we can disturb the ground below and break them out. Two guards stand on each side and Hermes masks our presence with a Mirage.

Bending the moonlight, he makes us invisible, and we swarm the guards as Odysseus feels along the rocky wall for the entrance.

With a wave of Absolute Light from my friend and a burst of Soul-Fire, we quickly dispatch the guards. I find a lone key hanging on the belt of the guard I killed and snap it off the leather tie.

Pity, they were low powered Elementals and perhaps on another day, we would have let them flee with their lives. But today, no one lives if they have aided in Calypso's captivity.

"Two minutes and we're gone." Hermes says as his eyes dart quickly across the legions of fighters below.

"I've got the entrance." Odysseus begins a small tremor that should break apart the earthen wards concealing the door. He pulls back his power, but the mountain continues to quiver and shake. His small vibration grows to a large one and the entire valley feels it.

The ground below us cracks and we slide down the embank-ment.

Fuck!

"Really, Odysseus?" Hermes swears under his breath.

"Sorry! This soil is a lot sandier than I expected."

The clash of metal and roar of Ares' army warns us as they ready themselves to fight us. Hermes unsheathes his sword.

Good fucking thing, because I was already halfway up the hill to retrieve my mate.

Blasting the exposed door with a ball of Fire, I step over the fragments of what remains. Letting my eyes adjust to the low light and smoke, I squint and follow the urges of my bond, trusting it will lead me to Calypso.

The agony filling the small space heats the fires that burn constantly within me, and I turn my hands red-hot.

I'm drawn to her as if I already knew her location in this small prison and quickly meet a cell at the end.

In a molten flash, I melt the iron doors and pull them from their hinges. The Thaumium metal cells restrict Elementals powers, but my fires are burning as hot as the forges of Vulcan where the alloy metal was crafted.

Pushing into the cell, the cowered and beaten woman that looks up at me steals the very breath from my lungs. In an instant, I would give her the last lungful of air if she needed it.

Her stola is dirty and tattered. Every inch of her skin is marred with dirt, scrapes, and bruises. The only space not covered are the two streaks where her tears have fallen.

The cuffs around her wrists are connected with a chain and I fist the key I snatched from the guard's belt.

Working to take in breath so I can speak to her, I move for her cuffs.

Shock busts through me when she grabs my arm, yanking me to her and kicking hard with both feet. I stagger backward and my emptied lungs are still unable to pull in a breath.

Calypso makes for the door but the clash of metal outside drives me to protect her from leaving the cave. I reach for the chain of her cuffs but she strikes me with it.

The burn is excruciating as the Thaumium metal slices my skin.

I love the feel of fire on my body, but this burn is unforgiving. I hiss and swear against the pain, and I work to breathe through the torment.

Odysseus rushes in and Calypso freezes.

Through their exchange, she blinks her beautiful blue eyes as understanding slowly surrounds her.

Dabbing the blood that runs from the cut over my eye, I hold my forearm to the wound. She turns, taking me in as if for the first time and I want to study the expressions running through her face.

Confusion, hope, denial. She filters through them all as if not wanting to let herself believe this is really happening.

"My name is Achilles, and I came with your brother to save you." I keep my voice steady as I discard a small ball of fire behind me to give us some light. My chest tightens when I see Calypso flinch and recoil away from the flames.

I fucked this up.

Cursing my recklessness, my impulsive nature is laid bare before her wounded gaze. She deserves better than this, better than a thoughtless warrior consumed by his own desires.

My face burns in shame at my rash entrance. Pat should be the one greeting her. Not me.

Gods dammit.

With the force of all the Titans, I turn away from her. Holding my hand out, I wait for her to see the key and take it. I notice how hard she works to ensure she doesn't touch me, and my eyes swell with angry tears.

Another burst of frustration pulls at me, and I eat up the distance to the next cell door, ripping it away and freeing Penelope. Another woman looks at me from within the cell.

Her leg is clearly broken, badly, and she's also received a beating recently. Aside from a limp, Penelope appears to be in good order.

Hearing the cuffs drop from Calypso's wrists, I sense the surge of wind before it enters the small cave.

As the currents of the realm swarm to her, Calypso's skin pales and her eyes roll back in her head. Dizzy and overwhelmed with the return of her powers, she begins to fall.

Like a burst of lightning, I move across the small cave and catch her.

The first touch of my skin on hers surges magma through my veins, igniting a primal fire within me. My soul-bond stretches within me, wanting to encase her in my aura and bond with her.

Exiting the cave, Hermes is a blur of Light and steel.

Calypso stirs and pushes out of my arms. Locking eyes with one man across the pass, he cuts his eyes to mine. They recognize each other and the wave of anger that rushes out of Calypso tells me this man is one of her captors.

He'll never fucking touch her again.

Hermes snaps his head toward us and then drives his sword deep into the ground. I couldn't hear the exchange but I'm guessing the siblings are speaking through telepathy.

Calypso raises her hands to the skies and a monster of her built up anger is born from the vortex of clouds above us. Reunited with her element, the Temptress calls upon the angry winds and together, they devour the army below. Her tornado skips down the pass, ingesting Ares's army and painting the swirl of wind red with their blood.

I pick out the agonizing screams of one individual as Calypso prolongs his demise.

Good. Her revenge has started. Together we'll find the rest until all her tormentors have been cast to the shadows of Elysium.

Pushing her waning strength into the funnel, Calypso falls.

Like gravity pulls me to her, I catch her before she can collide with the ground.

The feel of her frail body, limp in my arms and marred by her abusers, breaks open my heart. A plea, perhaps it's a promise, runs through every fiber of my Immortal being. A vow, that I will see through until the end of my time.

"I swear by the blood that courses through my veins and the fire that burns within my soul, I will stop at nothing to shield you from any harm that dares to threaten your existence."

Achilles

My heart races as the small goddess, tended to by her aunt, consumes my thoughts, each beat a painful reminder of my longing to comfort her.

Hermes managed to contact Athena outside the protective wards of the mountains, and I reached Pat through our bond.

Plans are underway to create distractions and mask our presence while Daphne and Atlas strengthen the wards around Delphi. The risk of Ares's wrath against other Immortals in retaliation for rescuing Calypso and Penelope is too great.

With a million tasks at hand and emotions peaking, I can no longer contain my words as Hermes, and I stand beneath a large tree. I confess the truth of our bond to Calypso.

She is still across the small pasture in the river with Penelope, unable to hear us. Her eyes reflect the trauma of her recent captivity.

"Hermes, I know this is difficult for you to accept, but Calypso's safety is my utmost priority now. I will do everything in my power to protect her."

Hermes' voice tightens with suppressed anger. "She's my sister, Achilles. I've always been the one to protect her. I don't need you to swoop in and play the hero now."

I clench my jaw at his stubborn response. This is exactly why I didn't mention the bond three months ago. Despite my growing irritation, I reflect on the countless times I asked Hermes about his missing sister.

Perhaps if he had not been so closed off, and shared his memories of her, my bond would have recognized her sooner. We could have found her sooner.

"I'm not trying to replace you, but you can't deny the fated bond between Immortals," I argue, tension crackling between us.

Hermes steps closer, his eyes flashing with a ring of aura around the blue iris in warning. My own power flares instinctively, interpreting the challenge of our unbonded connection as my powers respond to defend Calypso.

"Bond or not, you don't get to dictate what happens to her."

"She didn't get to dictate what happened to her for twenty years and you don't know what she endured in that cave; I do." As Hermes turns to walk away, I pull his arm back, forcing him to keep facing me.

"I don't care what you felt in that cave; that's my sister." Hermes holds me by my collar and our powers flare around us. Hermes radiates blue starlight, while my fire simmers dangerously close to the surface, emanating from my wide shoulders. "She'll take all the time she needs, and you'll be patient."

"I'll be patient, Hermes," I whisper, "but I won't stand idly by while she's in danger. I'll protect her, whether you like it or not." My gaze remains steely, resolved to do whatever it takes to safeguard my newfound mate.

Shoving Hermes away from me, I knock his shoulder as I pass. "I'll take the first watch."

"My Light Shield is cast and will tell me if anyone moves within a half-mile from us." Hermes calls back as I retreat into the night.

Throwing my arms wide, I walk away from my friend. "And yet, I'll still be taking the first watch."

❧ ❧

Hermes and I will be fine in a few days. The impacts of this tension are straining on Calypso, even though she's trying to hide her emotions. I see them flowing off her in torrents.

It takes all my power not to keep my gaze fixed on her. She keeps flicking her eyes to me and a river of emotions cascade from her aura.

Curiosity pulls her to me first, then revulsion pushes her away.

I swallow the knot in my throat when it happens a dozen times as we get ready to teleport back to Delphi. I should have been calmer when I first entered the cave, but my instincts consumed me.

I put my head in my hands, rubbing my face and squeezing my eyes tight. I just want to get home to Pat and bury myself in his presence. Apologize to him for the dipshit he's mated to because I've ruined our introduction with Calypso, and he'll have to suffer the consequences with me.

As the flash of the portal fades away, I stalk forward, keeping myself just ahead and at the edge of Calypso's view. I want her to be able to see me and the distance I put between us and hope she realizes it's for her comfort. Even though the space feels agonizing to endure.

The Commune has come to see the return of Apollo's daughter.

The way their gazes linger on her pisses me off. I want to burn their eyes and rob them of their sight forever for looking at her as if she is a spectacle.

"Find someone else to stare at and go about your day." I bark at the crowd forming along the wide path leading up to the center of Delphi. Some scurry about their tasks, while others roll their eyes at me.

That's fine, I'll gladly be the one to take their looks and judgment so long as Calypso doesn't have to bear the weight of them.

Patroclus stands at the threshold of our home, his face displaying a knowing look of sympathy and amusement. His light eyes hold me in his stare as my temper calms with his nearness. He looks over my injury caused by the hands of our fierce and frightened little siren.

"So, it could have gone better, I take it?" Pat is an expert in making light of a situation to alleviate tension.

"I deserve this." I roll my eyes as I reach his side. "I deserve this and a thousand more lashings. I'm sorry but I fucked this up."

Pat rubs his hand down my arm in a reassuring caress before he laces his fingers with mine. Just as I'm drawn to her, so is he. I watch Patroclus as he watches her walk up the path.

Their eyes meet, and while she holds her chin high and turns away first, he continues to watch. I see it, the second her presence roots into him, and just like me, she'll stay there forever.

Calypso disappears beyond the curve of the walkway, out of our sight. Pat looks back at me with eyes as bright as the crystal waters of the Mediterranean. The smitten look of utter contentment is on his handsome face, exposing both dimples.

I can't help but smile in return.

"So, not love at first sight," He jests. "But we'll get there." Using his hand, he sweeps a strip of my long locks behind my ear, and I run my thumb gently over his bottom lip.

I rub my nose against his tenderly, and he responds with an approving hum.

"I love you." I speak the words against his mouth before I pull him into me for a deeper kiss. My tongue sweeps across his with comforting ease and the tension in my tight shoulders relaxes with his warm touch.

"Give her time, that's all we can do for her now." After giving me another peck, Pat takes my hand and leads me toward the door to our home. "Now, let's go inside so I can take care of my Flame."

Returning to the Commune, a surge of worry grips me instantly as Pat mentions his time with Callie, working on helping her open up.** Although I'm glad she's on a healing journey, jealousy gnaws at me, wishing I could be part of her happiness. Her gaze still carries a wave of revulsion whenever it falls upon me.

Pat returns home, her scent clinging to him like a cloak, a bitter-sweet reminder of their time together.

As he embraces me, I find solace in inhaling their intertwined fragrances:the scent of a salty Mediterranean bonfire mixed with the fragrance of lemons and jasmine.

It's that scent that ignited the hailstorm of my wrath today as Hermes and I searched an abandoned citadel.

Patroclus senses the tension through our bond as I work to compose myself. He wants to know what happened. During the mission with Hermes, I shielded my fated connection to Patroclus. I didn't want to spoil his time with Callie, so I closed myself off.

Returning to Delphi we head to the Commune's security center and Medusa inspects my eye as Pat arrives with Callie.

"Tell me what happened, lover." Every word Patroclus speaks is laced with concern, though he maintains his composure in front of our unbonded mate.

"Paris still had her fucking nightdress." I feel a near-murderous rage and my hands tremble at my sides. "Her scent still lingered on it and that fucking bastard was still using it."

I lost control.

We were supposed to scout the citadel for signs of Hermes' secret goddess. He fears she is a captive and we thought understanding how Paris keeps his prisoners would help our search for her.

But when I saw that nightdress sitting on top of his workbench of knives, with fresh blood still sitting in the crevices of the rock-paved ground, I lost it.

Penelope had described the storm that sunk their ships and how Odysseus was separated from her and Callie. She explained those first few days of their captivity but nothing else.

Seeing the nightdress Calypso wore when she was captured sucked me into a vortex of disbelief. My trembling hand reached for it slowly. I was mildly aware Hermes was across the room, but the tattered article of clothing was a single beacon in total darkness.

Taking it in my hands, the faint scent of lemons and jasmine reached out to me like a ghost of Callie's captivity that was left behind.

It's as if a thousand flashes of Callie's torture bombarded me and I turned into an inferno. Hermes barely had time to teleport away from me before I unleashed a lake of fire across the empty castle.

Only the residue of my hatred for Paris lingered after the destruction.

During lunch with Hermes, our moods mirror the turmoil within us.

While he battles his nightmares, I'm consumed by thoughts of Paris, vowing to make him pay for Callie's torment.

"I made progress today with Callie," Pat communicates telepathically while everyone eats. With my arms crossed over my chest, I acknowledge Pat with a thin smile. I know he's trying to take my mind off Paris, but he'll plague me until he's dead. "Watch this."

I feel the small breeze wave by us and combine with Pat's seafoam aura before it wraps around Calypso. She feels it and something passes between them. He makes her smile with whatever was said and Calypso covers her face with her napkin to hide the joy he brings her.

She often does this. Like she feels as though she doesn't deserve to be happy, and the thought crushes me.

"She taught me how to speak to her using the Wind."

It takes all my effort to remain composed and hide my shock. I didn't realize that was possible for someone who was not a Siren. "Can anyone do it?"

Pat smiles when he tells me how she taught him, my spirits are lifted. The afterburn of destroying Paris' castle cools and I make plans for myself the rest of the afternoon.

I still come to the cliffs at Silver Strand to clear my mind but today I come to tame the Wind. Perhaps that is a bit lofty, but I'm determined. I have to focus my attention on something other than Paris and there is no other mystery greater to solve than finding a way into her heart.

The Wind is her element, and she can trust in it. If the Wind can help me scale the walls she's built around herself, then I'm not leaving these cliffs until the finicky element lets me speak to Callie, just like Pat.

How the fuck am I going to do this?

Standing at the edge of the cliffs, I think about that day when Callie's power surged across the realm beseeching help. The Winds carried the vision of her directly to Pat and me, not Hermes. The Elements know we are fated together and surely will be willing to help.

I flare my aura into a single flame that burns in the center of my outstretched palm.

I watch the little fire sway in the gentle breeze and pray upon the torrents of the four Winds.

"Wind," Is this how you start a conversation with an invisible element? I'm not sure so I just keep going. "I beg you to carry my words to Calypso. Tell her of my love, my devotion."

Still watching the flame, it stills in my hand as if the Winds of the realm ignore me. Burning steady with no soft currents to ruffle it, the little fire almost looks up at me with steadfast readiness for our next attempt.

With a deep breath, I try again. "Surely you can see how much she means to me. I know you care for her too."

This gets a reaction; I think.

The air beyond the cliffs seems to respond. It rises above the cliffs and thrums against my chest, catching my long hair in its waves before it dies down.

"You would deny me?" I cock my eyebrow. The slow-healing gash caused by Callie burning only a little with the movement.

With this, the currents stop completely. Not a single blade of grass rustles and even the waves below calm.

Okay, well that is not the right approach.

"Are you angry with me?"

A giant gust of air sweeps low to the ground and steals my footing. In an instant, I'm lying flat on my back against the rocky ground, clutching my stomach and gasping for air.

Son of a bitch. That fucking hurt.

"I'm going to mark that down as maybe." I try a humorous answer and it lands flat.

I feel the surge of air coming down like a giant fist of currents heading straight for me. Rolling to the side, the Wind slams into the ground where I was laying, sending a plume of dirt in all directions.

"I'll update that to a yes, then."

For the next hour, the Wind and I fight a battle of wills.

I taunt and poke with my words and the Wind either ignores me like a scorned lover or combats me like an angry warrior.

At the end of the second hour, frustration creeps into my voice as the stubborn force refuses to heed my call.

"Can't you see how much she means to me?" I yell across the cliffs, my words lost in the gusts that whipped around me.

With a heavy heart, I sink to my knees, defeated by the unyielding force of nature. My tears mingle with the salt spray as I pour out my soul to the wind.

"I swear on my life that I will always love and protect her," I vow, my voice filled with raw emotion. "I rushed into her cell to save her just as you rushed to her side the second those cuffs were removed from her body."

Recalling the surge of currents that stole her breath and made her dizzy as she absorbed the might of her Elemental power.

"You are no different than I am when it comes to her. Please, help me break through her barriers, help me show her the depth of my feelings."

I let my head fall to the ground and beat my fist on the dirt. The currents go still around me as if finally refusing to entertain this pitiful display of pleading any longer.

After a moment's pause, the winds shift.

The currents swirl and push against me and I right my posture. Sitting up and looking out over the cliffs, I see a vortex of white clouds grow closer.

Squinting my eyes, I realize it's not clouds, but a rush of feathers swirling in on the currents. I watch in awe as one delicate plume separates itself from the mass.

Swaying back and forth, it drops down as the rest of the feathers keep their cyclone around me. Landing gently in the palm of my hand, the Wind offers me a silent promise to help in my quest to win Calypso's heart.

Lifting the small feather to my mouth, I hold it against my lips. Thankful for the bargain struck with the element she commands, I raise the feather to the sky and the Wind carries it away from me.

"I love you, Calypso. And that is a promise that will never change."

Achilles

"**Free the slaves. I'm tearing down the citadel.**" Callie's words, spoken before her currents carry her to the castle, mark the last moment of peace before chaos reigns at Sardis.

The last six years have been terrible. I have no idea why I expected anything better tonight. But hope filled me when Hermes said Callie agreed to take the mission together, just the two of us.

We've never had any time alone together, and the knots formed in my stomach are signs of my nervousness. She still can't stand the sight of me and even tonight, she avoids looking at me if she can.

The Wind swirls around my wrist before it chases after her. A small sign of understanding that I've come to interpret over the past few years.

It was difficult to translate, at first.

After that day on the cliffs, when I argued with the Wind, we reached a truce. For Calypso, we would do anything. So, each time

I found a feather, I would push my love and intentions into it. Holding it up, a current of the realm would wrap around it and ferry it to her.

After several feathers, I never really knew if she was receiving them. One day, I saw the Wind return and dance before me. Rustling several leaves into a figure eight, they swirled in the excited current at my feet.

"Did she get the feather?" I asked.

The leaves danced with more vigor than before, and it made me smile. It was like an excited little puppy wagging its tail.

Another day, a different feather didn't make it to her. I watched as the Winds tried to get her attention with it. Using her element against itself, she flicked the feather out of her face with annoyance and the disappointed Wind let my token fall to the ground.

Dragging it back to me, the Wind lifted the feather back into the palm of my hand. It swirled around my wrist as if saying, "It's okay." And "Next time.".

I fixed the discarded feather to my leather necklace and Pat placed a heat shield around it for preservation.

The day Pat took Callie dancing in the clouds, it didn't go well in the end. She had a nightmare and he was locked inside the torment with her. I felt my mates suffering under the memory of her imprisonment.

Hermes and I battled a league of Ares' forces.

Torn between fighting with him or going to my mates, I looked to the skies around me.

A raging storm swept in from nowhere and I realized it was Calypso.

Rain burst from the skies above us and the torrents refused to give up for hours.

It was her despair.

As a metal sword clashed with my Flaming blade, I called upon the Winds.

"Go to them!" I begged to the tempest swirling above us. "Wake up, Patroclus!" I screamed down our bond.

I felt the Wind push through our door as it disturbed my protective shield around our home. Bringing a rush of white feathers, the Wind swirled around our bedroom as I yelled down the mating bond to Patroclus. "Go to her!"

My billow against the winds in our room ripped him from the nightmare and he was on his feet in an instant. As soon as he let me know he reached her door, I closed off our bond and pushed my frustration into the battalion before me.

It's what I did tonight at Sardis.

Callie refused to acknowledge me and flew on her Winds to the castle.

I fight against the troops that rush out to defend the city and make sure only refugees are able to flee the citadel. Every soldier who tries to escape meets death.

Sensing danger is approaching our mate, I spin behind me, finding Calypso on the wall of the citadel. Her powers are a tight swirl of ribbons around the castle and it's about to explode.

She's not paying attention to the Water Sirens behind her that have aimed their sharpened blades of Water at her back. Either that, or she doesn't care.

Like a raging flash of Fire, I am with her in a second. My Fire eats the Water Sirens weapons as if they are nothing more than steam, but I didn't account for her explosion of Wind.

I realize it the second she does, and we collide into each other. Holding onto her, the Wind carries us away from the blast.

"What the fuck was that?" She pushes against me, but I feel only her anger for my disruption as she stalks away into the night. She wasn't repulsed by me. For the first time, hope blooms in my chest.

We could have worked a little better together, I admit, but looking over the city, her reaction grates against my understanding and leaves me confused.

The citizens are free, and the citadel was destroyed. I don't understand why she is so angry and as seconds pass, I grow angry with her.

It seems like she's merely being stubborn at this point, refusing to acknowledge that she is my mate, just as much as Patroclus. For years, we have balanced on this delicate line together without ever talking about it. Bonding with Patroclus increased the feelings that pour off her and I've sensed the change in how she perceives me.

There is some prejudice she holds against me, but goddess knows she'll never admit what it is. I will wait for her for a thousand lifetimes, but gods dammit, she's going to talk to me tonight.

Ripping the rest of my tattered shirt and discarding it to the forest floor, I stalk after her.

The Winds form a path through her shield, leading the way to a darkened tavern where her irritation radiates from within.

Taking the leather tie from my neck, I wrap my hair in a tangled ball at the top of my head to keep it out of my face. With each step, my frustration grows and smoke billows in my wake.

I need to calm down but the second I enter the tavern, the heat in Callie's stare crumbles all my resolve. She meets my passion with her own and we collide into each other in a glorious explosion.

She jumps into my arms, and I can't devour her fast enough.

Dreaming of her taste for years, I need to consume her, to claim her for myself, and satisfy this starving bond.

Barely taking time to remove our clothes, she brings me to the heavens when she wraps her beautiful mouth around my cock.

Keeping my eyes closed, I beat my head on the door to keep myself from cumming. When I cum in her for the first time, it won't be in her mouth.

I pull her back into my arms. I want to lift her and let her bracket my head with her legs. I want her soaking pussy in my face so I can explore every inch of her with my tongue. I want to know if she tastes like sweet lemons or fragrant jasmine like the perfume that lingers around the Commune driving me insane with the ghost of her presence.

Our bonds decide for us and pull us together.

The first sensation of uniting with her rushes a wave of flames inside me that rips a groan from my throat. She's so tight and wet, perfectly griping me as I reach into her with my erection.

The Winds circle us as I fight to keep my Fire inside me.

We figured out early that Callie was tortured by the Flames of Hector and Paris. Patroclus and I have been careful to contain our element, so we don't thrust her into memories she is trying to heal from.

My bond reaches for her as I drive my cock in and out.

I'm desperate to feel her reach back for me. I just want to know that she has a willingness to bond. Even if it's not today. I'm okay going slow but the unknowing is killing me.

Her bond is as chaotic as her emotions and the unpredictable Wind that she commands. My bond waits for her, a patient thrumming between us, hoping for her longing to connect.

She comes, squeezing around me and scratching down my back. The burn of her scratches and the throbs of her pussy bring me to my own climax.

She doesn't open up and let me in. She holds back her bond, not wanting to mate with me.

The furnace of my passion for her turned cold in an instant, knowing she was only driven by the compulsions of her bond. Did I fuck things up again?

Horror coats my face at my actions as I watch her trembling body. She's closed herself off entirely from me and I can't interpret the dozen emotions that fly through the teary gaze in her eyes.

What if she didn't really want this? Will she regret me tomorrow?

I want to reach out for her, but I'm terrified to see her recoil away from me. Not when my heart is still pounding in my chest from making love to her. When my lips are still hot from the feel of her mouth on mine.

Without saying a word, and as tears spill over her blue eyes, Callie gathers her clothes. With a slam of the door behind her, I'm left standing alone in the dark tavern, unbonded to Callie.

Callie, Patroclus, and I stand outside a tavern much like the one we barged into after Sardis. This one is lit with warm yellow light, and I feel the fire dancing inside the large fireplace inside.

I look down at my mate as a gentle breeze billows her long platinum hair. A sly smile spreads on her face and I know she's thinking back to that night too. Meeting Pat's eyes, he grins wickedly, having heard all about our first time together in the abandoned tavern outside of the city we ransacked.

"Come on, we'll have a better time in this tavern than we did at the last one." Taking her hand, I pull her in front of me. I wrap my arm around her waist and nuzzle her neck.

"Oh, is that a promise?" She answers back sarcastically but leans her head to the side, giving me room to enjoy the feel of her skin on my lips.

Pat takes her hand and with a spin, he turns her into him. Their mouths are so close Callie opens her lips, expecting his kiss. "That's a promise, little siren." Leaving her wanting, Pat's smile widens, and he pulls her with him toward the tavern steps.

Holding the door for my mates, they enter in front of me. I smack Pat's ass, eliciting a wink as we walk inside.

The tavern owners bring us meat and mead. The stewed potatoes and crusty bread are especially delicious and as we wait for our room to be prepared.

Finished with her dinner, Callie pushes her plate back. Patroclus scoots her chair closer to his and leans his elbow on the back as she talks about our day. I can't keep my eyes off them and sit back in my chair, enjoying the sight of them together.

Reveling in our successful mission, I think about what I almost lost a century ago.

Coming back from Sardis without being mated to Calypso broke my heart. I felt my soul cracking as I feared she didn't want me.

I could never be selfish and demand it of her or expect Pat to live a life split between two mates.

I was going to leave.

Ready to let them live as a mated pair, I planned to tell Pat goodbye and return to Skane. The old Commune was nothing but ruins, but I could rebuild it.

I could put my energy and anger into restoring the old structures and make a new Commune. Brick by brick, I was ready to spend a few centuries bringing back the home of the Vikings.

But Callie came back. She fucking came back.

Showing up at our house with the small token I had been sending to her in her hands pulled my crumbling world back together. She twirled the feather and ran her fingers along the soft barbs in an absentminded attempt to soothe herself.

As I calmed the firestorm swirling in my soul, I confessed my contract with the Wind. She finally told me why she had resisted our bond and all Winds and Fires of the realm celebrated when our bonds accepted each other.

Now a hundred years later, we've moved past so many trials together and I'm the luckiest Flame that has ever existed to be mated with such amazing Immortals.

I watch Pat move a strip of Callie's hair behind her ear and I lavish the sight of her holding his hand to her face, enjoying the embrace a moment longer.

She kisses the inside of his palm before holding his hand in her lap. They lean forward and I watch the silhouette of their lips part as their tongues find their way to each other. Backlit by the fire, I consume the sight of my mates' affections and my dick pulsates, wanting to taste them both for myself.

Calypso guides Pat's hand between her legs and I watch the movement of his forearm muscles as he plays with her. Now my dick is basically screaming at me to get the fuck out of here or just take them both across this tavern table.

"Mmmm," Pat's deep voice slides into our thoughts, coated with seduction. "Our little siren is still hungry, lover."

Standing and turning to the tavern keepers, I demand our room.

A single brass key arcs across the tavern and I catch it in one hand.

Callie and Pat follow me as I take the stairs two at a time until I reach the top. Sliding the key into the hole, I open the door. Pat scoops Callie into his arms and ascends the stairs at the same pace. His eagerness makes her laugh and the brightness in his minty eyes pulls a smile to my face.

The mortal tavern doesn't have the sophistication of our Communes, with showers and constant hot water, but at least there is a pump to fill a large bath. Our element warms the water as we strip our clothes. With Callie back in his arms, Pat steps into the tub. Kneeling, my mates begin washing each other through strokes and kisses on each other's bodies.

A wave of my heat shields our room and barricades the fragile mortal door.

With lust-coated eyes, Calypso burns me alive with her gaze on my cock.

Gods, this woman.

I don't know what I did to deserve this bliss, but I thank the Fates each day for my mates.

She takes my hand and pulls me to her. Stepping into the tub, Pat and Callie turn their attention to me.

Their soapy hands and warm rags stroke my body.

Closing my eyes and tilting my head to the ceiling, I enjoy the sensations of their touch on my skin.

Pat kisses the line of my pelvis as Callie takes my dick in her hands. I groan as they lavish me, and Callie adds a kiss of her own to my other hip.

I watch my mates, enraptured as they keep their gazes fixed on each other. Opening their mouths, each of them lick the long length of my cock. The warmth of their wet tongues and their breath against me pulls another moan from me that bounces around the surfaces of the bathroom.

Pat reaches the tip of me, and he closes his eyes as his mouth forms a tight seal around my cock. He slides my length into him. His tongue massages me as his mouth sucks me. Calypso's grip on the base of my dick tightens and her other hand squeezes my balls.

She licks and sucks along my pelvis while she waits for her turn.

As Pat slides my erection out of his mouth, Callie is ready for a thorough taste of her own. Following Pat, she sucks me deep in her mouth until I reach the back of her throat.

I know how long and thick I am. She never fails to impress me with how deeply she can take me.

Her tongue swirls along my shaft in time with her suctions as she moves back and forth.

Pat sticks his finger in his mouth as his gaze fans the fires of desire burning inside me.

Reaching past my testicles, his finger glides between my ass, sliding easily inside me. Calypso picks up her tempo, matching her mouth and hand to the pace of her movements.

"Fuck me." I groan as my mates work to build my climax. "You're such a good siren, swallowing my dick so perfectly."

"Does our good girl deserve a reward?" Patroclus eases his other hand between Callie's legs, circling her clit as she rotates her pelvis.

My fingers thread through their hair and Callie grunts against my cock as Pat makes her come. The sensations of her pleasure thrum against my dick in her mouth as Pat's finger pulsates inside me. My mates stimulate me from each side, bring me to an intense orgasm as Callie swallows my cum.

"Stand up, handsome." I take Pat's hand and lick the taste of Callie off him. He stands, and our mouths meet, sharing her sweet juices between us. I hold his chin between my thumb and forefinger. "Now sit. Good little Flames deserve rewards too."

Pat sits on the edge of the large tub, his erection still hard and wanting release.

Taking Callie's hands, I help her stand. My mouth takes her breast and I graze my teeth along her nipple. "Are you ready to swallow another dick, little siren?"

I don't let her answer before my kiss devours her moans. My finger slides up the slit of her wet pussy and I feel her throb against me, wanting.

"Yeah, you're ready for your mates' cocks." I turn her around and Pat leans back.

His icy eyes stay fixed on our little siren's lips as her tongue moves across them. She runs her hands up the length of his muscular thighs as I tease the entrance of her pussy with the head of my dick.

I watch her. As she fills her mouth with Pat, I fill her tight hole with my dick.

Her pussy tightens around me as her mouth squeezes around Pat. He throws his head back as her deep moan vibrates against his shaft buried deep in her throat.

I fuck her softly so she can suck our mate's dick. I finger her clit as she works her mouth along him. The sight of his cock disappearing into her sweet mouth makes my balls tighten with the need to spill into her.

Callie comes first; always.

As her pussy clenches around me, I thrust into her harder. The callused tip of my finger pushes against her clit and she moans. Pat grabs the back of her head, steadying her as I pound into her.

The color of his rich skin against her light hair is as fascinating as his cock plunging into her mouth. He fists her locks as he grunts his own release into her, and she takes every drop greedily.

I come with my mates and the sensations of our pleasure roll down our bond, extending the waves of our climax as we ride each other to completion.

With an accomplished smirk, Callie turns to me. Pulling me by my neck, she drives her tongue into my mouth, sharing Pat's come with me. I squeeze her ass with my hand and devour the taste of our mate as she kisses me deeply.

Pat kisses her round ass before moving his lips to the small of her back. Standing, he kisses her shoulder and moves her hair to the side for a taste of her neck.

I turn Calypso to Patroclus. Wrapping her arms around him, Pat plunges his tongue into her waiting mouth.

Pulling up the drain and stepping out of the tub, I wrap a towel low on my waist.

The room is dark as the sun has set so I use my powers to ignite the candles along the expansive bedroom. I spark the logs in the fireplace and spread the heat through the room, warming it for Callie.

She meets me at the fireplace with a towel wrapped around her. Putting her in front of me, I rub her arms as she watches the fire.

She leans against me as I massage her shoulders, working out the tight muscles from today's battle. "That feels so good."

Looking at the candles, I ach to see the wax dripping down her beautiful ivory skin. I want to watch my flames kiss her flesh as I lick her pussy, warming her with my powers as I fuck her.

Callie still has nightmares of her time in captivity. Moments where her mind dips down into that well of darkness when she was raped and tortured by two Flames. Pat and I work to light up that dark space and keep her from falling back into it. Our Fires have become a sanctuary of peace and security, but we've not yet used our Fire for her pleasure.

The burn of the candles and the crackle of the fireplace ignite the desires in my mind to try.

Turning her to face me, I cup her cheek and look into her soft blue eyes.

"Can we try something tonight with you?" I rub my nose against hers and her tender smile is full of trust and contentment.

Pat joins us, placing a kiss on my bicep and rubbing his hand up Callie's thigh, breaching the hem of her towel. I move my arm to pull him into our embrace and we surround our little siren with our presence. Reaching behind her, I take a candle from the mantle.

The flame dances in her eyes and she looks between Pat and me. She rakes her nails up the front of our towels, barely scratching along our dicks that harden at her touch.

"Yes."

"We can stop anytime you're getting uncomfortable," Pat adds as he places a gentle kiss on her temple. She smiles and nods.

"Pick a safe word."

She toys with the edge of the candle, keeping her finger just outside the melted wax as she thinks.

Smiling, she answers. "Oranges."

Pat chuckles and I feel lost on the joke.

"Something I should know about oranges?" I ask with my scarred eyebrow raised.

My mates cut their eyes to each other and laugh again. "Just a flavor we both enjoy." Pat winks at me as he takes Callie's hand.

Leading her to the large bed, he unwraps her towel.

"Let's start with a massage," Pat says low with his lips pressed against her neck. I watch Callie shiver as if Pat's deep voice rolls down her body.

Taking her hand and placing it low with her palm up. I notice the tremor in her fingers and my eyes snap to hers.

"Are you nervous?"

"A little," Callie bites her cheek, looking down. Her long, dark lashes sweep the tops of her blushing cheeks. "But I want to try."

"We're going to take care of you," I reassure her.

When she nods in agreement, Pat holds the creme-colored soy candle high above her. Slowly, he drips a small amount on the palm of her hand. She watches the wax drip, and we watch her reaction when it touches her skin.

Placing the candle down, Pat takes her hand in his and rubs the drying wax, using it to massage her. She smiles slightly, enjoying the feeling and Pat places a kiss on her palm when he's finished.

I sit her on the edge of the bed with my candle. Kneeling before her, I take her foot and place it on my leg. Dripping the wax down her ankle, I study her.

Her chest rises with her deep breaths, and the gentle tremor is still present. But when the warm wax touches her skin, her eyes dilate. As the wax cools, her nipples harden.

That's my good girl.

Warming my hands with my power, I massage her foot, rubbing the soy wax until it's gone, using the oils it leaves behind to please my mate. I kiss along the arch of her foot, moving up to her ankle. Spreading her leg, and warming my lips, I kiss her knee and run my hot tongue up the slit of her pussy.

She moans, letting her head fall back and enjoying the sensation of the warm temperature on her center.

I keep my eyes fixed on her when she lifts her head to look at me. "We would never hurt you."

She nods in agreement, and I know she trusts us completely.

Pat eases her to lay down on her stomach and we kneel on each side of her. We rub the spot on her skin first so she knows where to expect the wax. Holding our candles high, we drip the melted wax, and it cools slightly as it falls to her beautiful skin.

Her muscles tighten for a moment, then as our warm hands rub her back, she relaxes.

Pat takes his candle and without warning this time, drips wax at a lower range onto her round bottom. I work her shoulders as he kneads her plump cheeks. We lavish her with praise and, like the wax, she melts under our touch.

Pat slides between her legs and she eases them apart.

He lets the melted wax drop so it runs down the crack of her ass and the line of her pussy. She moans as Pat uses his fingers to rub the wax along her and I hear his fingers slide along her slick center.

"You're soaking wet, Siren. Are you enjoying this?" he asks.

She nods her head as her mouth parts.

"Use your words, little siren." Pat slides two fingers into her and she arches her back.

"Yes!"

"Good, baby." Pat takes his fingers out and Callie catches her breath at the loss. Running his wet finger along my lip, he licks off the taste of her and then kisses me.

Turning her over, I sit back on my heels between her legs. Pat and I both removed our towels, and our cocks are hard and ready for our little siren. I place my candle on the table, but Pat keeps his.

"Can I touch you with my flames?" I hold her gaze as I keep my hands at my sides.

She bites her lips and nods her head.

"Words, little siren." I run my finger along the slit of her pussy with a featherlight touch.

"Yes, I want you to touch me with your flames." she answers in a breathy response.

I lean forward, placing my hand next to her head, and kiss her. "Tell me what your safe word is again."

"Oranges."

"Good girl." A small flame dances on the tip of my finger. "Blow it out, baby. I want you to know, you are the one in control here."

Her lips form an "o" but I pull my finger back. "Not with your mouth. I have plans to fill that with my dick." I lick her lips and she opens them, wanting my tongue in her mouth but I don't give her the satisfaction. "Now, blow it out."

I bring my finger back to her and she surges a small gust of her powers, snuffing out my flame.

"Such a good girl for me." I draw the words, slowly running the tip of my hot finger down her lip, then her chin, and finally down the center of her chest.

Callie arches her back and Pat drips wax onto her pert nipple.

Rubbing her attentive bud between his fingers, she closes her eyes and enjoys our hot exploration of her body.

"Eyes on me, baby." I take her chin and look at her until I see her rich blue eyes looking back at me. Desire and longing have turned them into a rich shade of sapphire. With her long hair splayed along the pillow and the rosy hue on her cheeks, she is striking.

"You are so beautiful." I reward her with the kiss she longed for a moment ago. She grunts as I dive into her with my tongue, and kisses me back fiercely.

I stick Callie's finger in my mouth and swirl my tongue around it. She watches me mesmerized and curious about what I'm doing. Igniting my power, her finger carries my gentle flame, letting it burn only a second before I snuff it out.

Taking her finger, I rub circles on her clit. The warmth from her finger heating her clit.

"Do you like it?"

"Yes, it's warm and it feels so good," Callie answers, rolling her head to the side and closing her eyes enjoying the sensations.

"Mmmm Pat, our good girl remembered to use her words." I adjust my position between her legs again. "Time for another reward."

She's so wet, I can smell the heat of her arousal and my mouth waters needing to lap up every drop.

Pat licks and sucks the tender spot on her hip and she moans in response. Pulling away, he ignites the spot and blows it out quickly before placing a kiss on the spot.

Pushing her legs apart, I lavish her pussy with a lingering, slow lick.

Callie lifts her head wanting to see. She loves watching me devour her.

Placing a kiss on her clit, I ignite the gentle flame, allowing it to burn a second longer than before. Just when I know the fire's heat flashes against her, I snuff it out and ravage her.

I suck and roll her clit, flicking my tongue across the tender bud as her hips buck against me. Pat takes her nipple between his teeth and pinches the other between his fingers.

Her nerves are ignited, stimulated by our element, heightening the sensations, and bringing her quickly to a hard orgasm.

I hold her legs open as I pillage her with my mouth. Lapping up the taste of her orgasm, I ease away only when I sense the muscles in her thighs relax.

I place kisses along her body until I meet her mouth. It's a soft and gentle kiss as I hold her in my embrace.

Rubbing my nose against hers, I'm proud of her bravery.

"Do you want some more, our hungry little siren?"

Tomorrow we march on Troy. As the night wears on and sleep eludes me, the gentle sound of my mates breathing keeps me calm. Bathed in the white light of the moon, Achilles, and Calypso sleep peacefully. As tension keeps sleep from reaching me tonight, I can't help but reflect on the journey that brought us to this moment.

It wasn't easy, but every second was worth it to see the love that now blooms between us, and to know that we are finally together as we were meant to be.

A lifetime ago we embarked on the mission to rescue Calypso from Ares and the princes of Troy, unaware of the fateful bonds that awaited us. The road has been long and demanding, filled with challenges and obstacles that tested our strength and resolve. But through it all, we survived.

I never lost faith that Callie and Achilles would find their paths together.

While it was difficult for Callie to admit, their love for each other and their unwavering determination guided them forward. Three links of a solidified chain, we became an unstoppable force of three souls whose hearts beat as one.

Callie shifts, turning to face me and scoots close into Achilles. His arm is wrapped around her waist, and he senses her shifting movements. Our ever-protective Flame pulls her in tighter and buries his nose in her hair. Releasing a deep sigh, they settle back into their deep slumber.

I'm proud of them, more than words can express. They've faced darkness and emerged victorious, their love shining brighter than any beacon in the night. And now, as they lay here in each other's arms, I can't help but feel a surge of gratitude for the love that binds us together.

Callie's hand rests on the mattress and I carefully slide my hand under hers. At my touch, her grip hardens, and I close my fingers around her, holding her steadfast as she sleeps.

Tomorrow, we march into battle once again, and the fear gnaws at my insides like a relentless beast. I know the risks we face, the dangers that await us on the battlefield, and I can't help but worry for the safety of my mates. But even in the face of uncertainty and danger, I will stand by their side, ready to protect them with everything I have.

I make a silent promise to myself and to them. I vow to always look over them, to protect them with every fiber of my being, for as long as I draw breath and forever after.

"Sleep well, little siren." I place a soft kiss on her hand. "Until tomorrow."

Acknowledgements

I just want to thank all the fans who love The Unforgotten Flame.

That little novella has such a dear space in my heart and healed a great deal of pain for me. I could not be more proud of Callie's story and you all deserve another perspective on some of the key moments of the heartbreaking story of pain, love and loss.

Thank you for your continued support and belief in me.

Until tomorrow,
Rebekah Sinclair

www.ingramcontent.com/pod-product-compliance
Lightning Source LLC
Chambersburg PA
CBHW061553310726
48972CB00008B/2733